Indian Ghost Mystery

by Bonnie Highsmith Taylor

Cover Illustration: Dea Marks
Inside Illustration: Dea Marks

Dedicated to Susan Sexton

About the Author

Bonnie Highsmith Taylor is a native Oregonian. She loves camping in the Oregon mountains and watching birds and other wildlife. Writing is Ms. Taylor's first love. But she also enjoys going to plays and concerts, collecting antique dolls, and listening to good music.

Printed in the United States of America. For information, contact
Perfection Learning® Corporation
Phone: 1-800-831-4190
Fax: 1-712-644-2392
1000 North Second Avenue, P.O. Box 500
Logan, Iowa 51546-0500.

Paperback ISBN 0-7891-5170-7
Cover Craft® ISBN 0-7807-9317-x
Printed in the U.S.A.
6 PP 06

Contents

1

Sent Packing

The most exciting thing in my life happened when Mom was expecting. I don't mean it was exciting that Mom was going to have a baby. That is unless you think that living with a crazy woman is exciting. Because that's exactly how Mom acted that spring.

Mom was sick a lot. And we only had one bathroom in the house. And she screamed at us over every little thing. And she ate weird stuff—like pudding with mustard on it.

One morning, Mom got me up an hour early. She sent me to the store for a can of olives. And when I got back, she took one look at the can and went nuts.

"They're pitted!" Mom yelled. "And I wanted to suck the pits!"

Then, Mom sat down and cried.

Dad said that after the baby was born, Mom would be her old self again. I could hardly wait.

But—if Mom hadn't been expecting a baby, Louie and I wouldn't have gotten on her nerves. Then Dad wouldn't have sent us to Grandma and Grandpa's for summer vacation. And if we hadn't gone to Grandma and Grandpa's, the most exciting thing in my life wouldn't have happened.

Besides, I never would have met Johnny Boyd.

Johnny Boyd was not the only boy in my life. I'd had my share of boyfriends. In kindergarten, there was Russell Anderson. But then he wet his pants on the school bus.

Then, from first grade through fourth grade, I liked Jeffrey Ober. Jeffrey was the cutest boy in the whole school. Totally terrific! But there was only one thing wrong with our relationship. No one knew about it but me.

I'm not sure if Johnny Boyd was as totally terrific as Jeffrey. Especially in the "cute" department. But Johnny was okay. He certainly was different from any boy I had ever known.

So I was glad that Louie and I were sent packing.

Louie is my little brother. He's seven. And he doesn't act too bright at times. Sometimes he's rotten too. But he's the only brother I have. And I guess I kind of like him—most of the time. And then, sometimes I can't stand him!

I'm 12 and my name is Alice Martha Turner. Isn't that awful? I was named after Mom's two aunts. They must be at least 75 years old!

I go to school with girls who have names like Lisa, Michelle, Lori, Tara, and Mia. And I'm the only one with a stupid, old-fashioned name. Of course, there's Dorothy Blake. But she's called Dori, which sounds really cool.

I have a secret, though. My name is Alice Martha only when I'm around other people. When I'm all alone, my name is Melanie Renee.

Sometimes I'm a model. Sometimes a great actress. Sometimes a famous singer.

Can you imagine being a model, actress, or singer with a name like Alice Martha?

Melanie Renee is so much better! It sounds like tinkly music.

Every doll I ever owned was named Melanie Renee.

Even the little dancing doll on top of my music box had that name.

Once, I had a beautiful goldfish named Melanie Renee. But Louie traded it off to his friend Peter for a toy car.

I was sick in bed with the measles. So I didn't find out about it for a week. By then, it was too late. Peter had traded it to Gary. Gary had traded it to Mark. And Mark's cat had eaten it. That was one of the times I couldn't stand my brother.

In real life, I even look like an Alice Martha. I'm an average student who looks like an average student. I'm too tall, with freckles and stringy, drab brown hair that won't stay combed. So I escape from myself through books and fantasy. It's because I have to—not because I want to.

Alice Martha! What a dull name! I hate it! And it doesn't help matters any when Dad calls me Al.

Mom calls me Alice and says the name fits me. My two great-aunts, Alice and Martha, call me Alice Martha.

"Remember, Al," Dad said the day he was driving us to Grandma and Grandpa's. "It's up to you to keep an eye on your brother. You know, keep him out of trouble."

At that moment, I was Princess Melanie Renee. And I was on my way to my royal wedding. So Dad had to repeat what he had just said.

"Do you understand?" Dad asked. "Mom and I are depending on you to keep a close eye on Louie."

"Uh-huh," I mumbled.

"Don't let him get into any trouble," said Dad. "And don't let him cause any trouble."

"Right," I sighed.

As if Dad had to remind me. Keeping Louie out of trouble had been my job ever since Louie had learned to walk. Right now he was jumping all over the front seat, chattering his silly head off.

"Can I help Grandpa milk the cows?" Louie said. "Can I drive the tractor?"

Nobody answered him. We usually didn't. Most of the time, he didn't seem to notice.

"I want you to help your grandmother around the house, Al," Dad said. "It was nice of them to agree to keep you for the summer."

I had to admit, it really was nice of Grandma and Grandpa. Spending the summer on the farm would be neat. We usually only visited there in the winter—at Thanksgiving and Christmas.

And getting away from Mom for a while would be a relief. I was pretty positive though that Louie was the one who was driving her up the wall. You didn't have to be pregnant to go out of your mind around him.

Mom and Dad say Louie is hyper. I guess that's as good an excuse as any.

I was beginning to think we would never get to the

farm. But finally, Dad turned off the highway onto a bumpy gravel road.

"Well, there it is, kids," Dad said. "You can see the top of the barn through the trees."

My heart jumped right up into my throat when I saw it. It was so much prettier in the summer than in the winter.

A creek ran along the edge of the trees. I'd never noticed it before. The pasture, so smooth and green, looked like a golf course. And some of the fruit trees were blooming.

As we got closer, I could see the chickens in the chicken yard. And clothes were hanging on the line.

Grandma was the only person I'd ever known who hung clothes outside to dry. Even in the winter. She didn't own a clothes dryer. And she said she never would.

Grandma and Grandpa must have heard us coming. When we pulled into the driveway, they were standing in the yard, smiling and waving.

Grandpa is awfully skinny. And it looked as though he'd lost another ten pounds. Grandma looked as though she had found it.

The best word for Grandma is "cute." Even if she always did scare me just a little. She's short and plump and doesn't wear any makeup, except a little powder. She can be smoochy and stern all at the same time.

Louie and I nearly got hugged and kissed to death. Even Dad got his share.

The first thing Grandma said was, "Edward Turner! Are you so hard up you can't afford to get your son a decent haircut?"

Dad laughed. "All the boys wear their hair that way, Mom," he said.

"Not around here," Grandma snorted. "No grandson of mine is going to look like that. I'll give him a decent haircut."

I flinched as she turned toward me. I was wearing blue jeans and a T-shirt. Luckily, it was just one of my plain T-shirts.

"Jeans, huh?" Grandma said. "Well, jeans have their place—especially on a farm. But I like to see girls look like girls. I hope you brought some dresses."

I hadn't. Just shorts and jeans. Mom had said we probably wouldn't be going anyplace where I'd need a dress.

"I don't know what this world is coming to," Grandma went on. "Boys want to look like girls. And girls want to look like boys."

Grandpa just sort of grinned. He looked happy to see us—bad haircut, jeans, and all. Grandpa never got upset about much of anything.

After the biggest, most delicious lunch I'd ever eaten, Dad left. He said he had to get back to Mom.

He'd promised to paint Louie's old crib and high chair for the new baby.

Mom wanted them painted pink. She was hoping for a girl. I don't think she could take another Louie. But she and Dad had finally settled on yellow.

The dust from Dad's car was still just settling to the ground. Grandma didn't waste any time. She plopped Louie down on a stool and started whacking at his hair.

Louie didn't move a muscle. I don't think he even breathed. He looked scared to death. And no wonder, the way Grandma was mumbling with every snip.

I had to smother a laugh when she finished. Louie slid down from the stool. His head was hanging way down. He looked just like a whipped puppy. I'd never seen him with such short hair. He really looked funny. And it didn't help that one side was shorter than the other.

Grandma put away her haircutting tools. Then she looked me up and down. I held my breath.

"I've got some nice material," Grandma said finally. "I'll make you some dresses later."

"A long one?" I cried. "Clear to my ankles?"

Grandma looked at me sharply. She must have thought I was being sassy. "That's not a bad idea," she said. "A lot more ladylike than wearing pants all the time."

I'd never had a long dress because Mom didn't think they were right for me. If I'd been Melanie Renee, long dresses would have been right for me.

Grandpa took Louie and me on a tour of the farm. We petted the cows, Buttercup and Daisy. Louie chased Daisy's calf all over the place, trying to pet him. Grandpa said the calf wasn't used to little boys.

"You can pet him later," Grandpa said to Louie. "When I close him in the barn at feeding time."

Poor calf, I thought.

Later, Louie sat on the tractor seat and pretended to drive. "Vrooom! Vrooom!" he yelled at the top of his lungs.

Chickens scattered in all directions. Grandpa clapped his hands over his ears and grinned. "It's a tractor, Louie. Not a motorcycle," he said.

When Louie finished on the tractor, we went to see the pigs. One of them had new babies. And then we saw the rabbits. They all had new babies. Then we visited the old horse. Next we saw the ducks, geese, and chickens.

Grandpa, Louie, and I walked through the orchard. I smelled the blossoms and skipped along the sandy bank of the creek. Grandpa puffed a little as he tried to keep up with Louie and me. Finally we stopped to rest.

"It's sure a big farm," Louie said, breathing hard.

"It's not as big as it was when your dad was a boy," said Grandpa. "Your grandma and I didn't need a lot of land after the family was grown and gone. So we sold part of it to a logging company. And they use it for tree planting."

Grandpa pointed off in the distance. Louie and I looked and saw row after row of little evergreen trees.

"Wow!" shouted Louie. "Look at all the little Christmas trees!"

Grandpa laughed. "That's what you call a tree farm, Louie," he explained. "Those little trees were hand-planted. They grew from seeds from the most perfect trees in the forests. In a few years, they'll be as big as the trees that were cut down years ago. That was back when this land was cleared for farming."

"As big as those giant trees growing up there?" Louie asked. He waved toward the land in back of Grandpa's farm.

"Yes, Louie," Grandpa answered. "As big as the trees on Indian Hill Game Refuge."

"Game Refuge?" Louie asked. "You mean like a park? How come there's a park way up there? And what's a refuge?"

Grandpa winked at me and rumpled Louie's hair. What was left of it, that is.

"Don't be so dumb, Louie," I said. "A game refuge is a place where wild animals are protected. Where they can live and not be hunted or bothered in any way." Our class had studied all about game refuges.

"Smarty," Louie said.

"Your sister is right," Grandpa said. "Anyone caught hunting or trapping on that land would be in a lot of trouble."

"But why is it called Indian Hill?" I asked.

Grandpa sat down on a big rock under an oak tree. He took off his hat, cleared his throat, and took a deep breath. I figured he was getting ready for a long story. So I settled myself on the ground at his feet. And Louie did the same.

"A long time ago," Grandpa began. "It was way over a hundred years ago. Only Indians lived here.

"After a while, a few white settlers began to drift in. The Indians didn't really like that. But they soon saw that the white folks meant them no harm.

"Most of these settlers were from a religious group. And they wanted to teach religion to the Indians.

"Well, their teaching didn't go over too well," Grandpa continued. "But the white folks stayed on anyway. And they went about their farming and building their homes."

Grandpa pulled his big handkerchief out of his back pocket. Then he wiped his forehead.

"Well," Grandpa continued. "Things went pretty well. That is until the Indians started getting sicknesses from the white folks—common diseases like measles and chicken pox. The Indians hadn't suffered from these diseases before. And a lot of the Indians got sick and died.

"One young brave lost his whole family to the measles," Grandpa continued. "He left his village and went to the white settlement to seek revenge for his people. But when he reached the settlement, he was very sick from the measles too."

I could tell Louie was as interested as I was. I'd never seen him sit still for any story. Grandpa was a good storyteller.

"Most of the white folks wouldn't have any part of that sick Indian," Grandpa continued. "But a young minister and his wife took him in. And they nursed him the best they could. But in spite of everything they did, the boy's body couldn't fight off the strange illness.

"When the young brave died, the minister picked a spot on top of that hill to bury him. And he gave the boy a white man's funeral.

"But the young brave's people were upset when they heard about it," Grandpa said. "They said without a proper Indian burial, the boy would never rest. He would roam forever."

Louie looked at me wide-eyed.

Grandpa continued. "The settlement never was the same after that. Crops failed. And before long, most of the settlers had moved on.

"Later, the government sent the tribe to a reservation," Grandpa finished the story. "Legend has it that the Indian brave's ghost is still seeking revenge. And to this day, a lot of people won't set foot on Indian Hill."

I had goose bumps all over me when Grandpa finished.

"Have you ever seen his ghost?" Louie whispered.

"Nope," said Grandpa. He stood up and put on his hat. "I don't expect to ever see it either." He kind of chuckled. "You can't see a ghost if you don't believe in them. But it's a good story. A darn good story."

As we walked back to the house, I couldn't help looking over my shoulder at Indian Hill. It looked so pretty and peaceful. So very peaceful.

2

The Farm

Grandma and Grandpa's farmhouse was really old. Grandpa's grandfather had built it. But it was still in great shape. Grandpa always kept it in good repair.

The house was three stories tall. And one of the upstairs bedrooms had a fireplace in it. I'd never seen a bedroom with a fireplace in it before. Dad said the room had been Grandma and Grandpa's bedroom when he was a boy. And Dad and his brother and sister had been born in that room.

I thought it must have been fun growing up in this old house. It had lots of staircases. And the closets were as big as regular rooms.

But the house had become too much for Grandma and Grandpa to keep up. So they only used the two downstairs bedrooms.

There was a television in the living room. But we learned later that they didn't watch it very much. Grandpa liked the Friday-night fights. And Grandma watched an afternoon cooking show. And they both watched the evening news.

"You two can share the spare room," said Grandma. "It's a big room. And you'll each have your own bed."

Neither of us would have dared to argue with Grandma. But she was acting as if we were.

"It won't hurt you one bit to share a room," Grandma continued. "And I don't see any sense in opening the upstairs. Not for the short time you'll be here."

I wasn't sure I liked the idea of sharing a room with my brother. But after we had our baths and went to bed, I decided it wasn't bad. At least on the first night. In fact, I think I would have been a little lonesome in a room by myself.

Grandma and Grandpa went to bed at the same time we did, a little before 9:00.

I couldn't believe a room could be so dark. There wasn't a ray of light anywhere. And it was quiet as a tomb.

A corner streetlight shone into my bedroom window at home. And I was used to the sound of cars driving by. This silence was awful!

Louie was already getting homesick. "Do you think she's glad we're gone?" he asked. His voice trembled a little in the dark.

"Who?" I asked, even though I knew who he was talking about.

"Mom, dummy," Louie said. "Do you think she's happy to have us out of the house?"

"Of course not," I said. "That's silly."

But I wondered too. She'd seemed in an awful hurry to pack our clothes. And after dinner tonight, we'd discovered she hadn't remembered to pack our toothbrushes.

"Then how come she was so mean to us?" Louie wanted to know.

"She wasn't mean to us," I said in her defense. "It just seemed that way." I explained as best as I could. "I guess being pregnant isn't easy. It makes you feel funny. And you get cranky."

"Grandma's cat, Callie, is pregnant," Louie said. "And she isn't cranky. She's as nice and friendly as can be."

"She probably doesn't even know she's pregnant." I sighed. "Now let's go to sleep."

I heard Louie sniffling a little. But he finally started snoring.

I felt a little like sniffling myself. Sure, I was looking forward to spending the summer on the farm. But I missed home as much as Louie. Maybe if I got to know Grandma a little better . . .

It seemed as though I had just dozed off. Suddenly, I woke with a start. Louie and I sat bolt up in our beds at the exact same time.

"What's that?" Louie yelled. "Alice, what is that noise?"

I listened, whispering to my brother to do the same. The noise filled the room again, only louder this time.

"It's a rooster," I giggled. I tried to pretend I had known all along what it was. "It must be morning."

"How can it be morning when it's dark outside?" Louie complained. "And I'm so sleepy?"

It was just barely starting to turn light outside. But I could hear Grandma banging pots and pans around in the kitchen. I couldn't complain about the silence now.

Louie and I went into the kitchen without even getting dressed.

"Well, good morning," Grandma said. "It's about time you two got up. I thought you were going to sleep till noon."

I looked at the clock on the wall over the stove. It was twenty minutes after five. No wonder they went to bed so early, I thought.

"Where's Grandpa?" Louie asked.

"He's out in the barn milking," Grandma said. "Where do you think? You think cows milk themselves?"

"I wanted to help!" Louie shouted. "Grandpa promised."

"Well, you can't help just standing there," Grandma said. "So get going!"

Louie tore out the back door. "Wait for me, Grandpa!" he shouted as he ran. "I'm coming! Wait for me. I'll help you!"

"Get back in here and get some clothes on!" Grandma called.

But it was no use. Louie was halfway to the barn.

"That boy," Grandma grumbled. But I'm sure I saw her grin as she turned back to the stove.

I helped Grandma with breakfast by buttering the toast and setting the table. I thought that the best part about this summer vacation would be eating. Grandma was an excellent cook.

At home, we'd been eating hamburgers, tacos, hot dogs, and lots of pizza. I didn't think I'd ever be able to look a pizza in the face again.

It didn't help either that sometimes Dad would try cooking dinner. That usually turned out worse than eating fast food.

The breakfast plates were heaped with ham and fried potatoes. Grandma was putting scrambled eggs onto the table when Grandpa and Louie came in. And was my brother ever a mess! His bare feet were covered with mud—or cow manure. Yuck! Gross!

Even if I am a city girl, I knew it was pretty dumb to run around in a barn without shoes.

On top of that, Louie's pajamas were soaked with milk. And his hair was full of hay.

Grandpa chuckled. "Meet my new farmhand, folks," he said. "Louie got so much milk on himself that the calf thought he was its mother." Grandpa shoved Louie toward the bathroom. "You'll get the hang of milking before long. Now go wash your hands. And your feet!"

I followed Louie into the bathroom to wash up for breakfast.

"Boy, you should have seen that crazy calf sucking my pajamas," he giggled. "I thought it was going to eat them right off me."

I giggled too. I wished I could have seen my brother milking a cow—in his pajamas and bare feet!

After breakfast, I helped Grandma do the dishes and clean up the kitchen. Louie helped Grandpa outside. I don't know how much help he was. But when they came back in a little after 10:00, he looked as though he had done a full day's work.

Louie was grimy from one end to the other. And his hair was slicked down to his head from sweating.

"Look, Alice," Louie said proudly, holding out his hand. "A blister. Grandpa says it will turn into a callus like his."

Maybe if Grandpa keeps him busy, I thought, he'll stay out of trouble. Then I won't have to keep an eye on him every minute.

"I've got a few things to pick up in town," Grandpa said as he sipped a cup of hot coffee. "You two want to go along?"

"All right!" howled Louie. "I do!"

I said yes too, but a lot more quietly. "Are you going too, Grandma?" I asked.

Grandma said she had to stay home. This was her day to bake bread. But she told us to go along. She wrote a list of things for us to buy in town, including toothbrushes.

As we backed out of the driveway in Grandpa's old pickup, Grandma called loudly from the porch. "You keep a close watch on those children, George," she shouted. "You hear me?"

"I will," Grandpa called back.

"How could he help hearing her?" Louie whispered to me. "She yells louder than Mom."

I poked Louie in the ribs. Grandpa looked straight ahead and pretended not to hear.

Willowdale had first been settled 125 years ago. It was a funny-looking little town. On one side of the narrow, bumpy street, the sidewalk was made out of wooden planks. Grandpa told us that the sidewalk, general store, and a few other buildings were nearly all that was left of the original town.

"People come from all over to see this town," Grandpa said. "There aren't too many like it left. They even shot a Western movie here some years back."

"Really?" said Louie. "That's super. Wait till I tell my friends. Hey, is there a saloon?"

"Yes, there is," Grandpa said. "It's right over there across the street."

The saloon looked just like the ones in Western movies. It even had swinging doors. If it ever had been painted, the paint had all worn off from the weather.

There were two long benches on the wooden part of the sidewalk. Several old men were sitting there. Some were talking. Some were dozing. And some were just looking around.

After we finished our shopping in the general store, we sat on a bench. Grandpa talked to some of the men while Louie and I ate ice cream bars.

Willowdale was nice and cozy. It was so quiet. No tires squealing. No horns honking. No buses roaring. It was a lot different from back home. I decided that I liked Willowdale a lot.

A big, shaggy dog came lumbering down the sidewalk. He stopped in front of each old man, including Grandpa. And they each gave the dog a pat on the head. He sniffed Louie and me a couple of times. Then he went on his way.

All of a sudden, it wasn't quiet anymore. The

window in the saloon exploded! Glass flew out into the street, followed by a chair.

A moment later, the door swung open. A man flew out and landed on the wooden sidewalk.

A man wearing a white apron stood in the doorway shaking his fist. "And stay out!" he roared. "Until you can keep a civil tongue in your mouth!"

"Yipes!" Louie exclaimed. He punched me on the arm and smeared ice cream on my sleeve. "Just like on TV, huh, Alice?"

I was too scared to answer.

The man lying on the ground looked terrible. He was moaning and squirming all over the place. He seemed to be in a lot of pain.

The man staggered to his feet. Another man—short, fat, and red-faced—came out of the barbershop next to the saloon.

"That you making all that racket, Ralphie-boy?" the fat man asked. He held out a pudgy hand to the fellow he had called Ralphie-boy. "Might have known I couldn't turn my back on you for a minute."

"Just a misunderstanding," said Ralphie. "Nothing serious."

Ralphie-boy looked right at us and grinned. Blood was running down his chin. I edged a little closer to Grandpa.

The fat man helped Ralphie into a battered green pickup. It was parked at the curb in front of the barbershop. A moment later, it clattered down the street and out of town.

Louie ran out into the street to look in the direction the pickup had gone. He pulled an imaginary gun out of an imaginary holster and yelled, "Pow! Pow! Pow!" But Grandpa made him come back and sit down.

"That's the fellow that's been staying out at Lacy's place, isn't it?" one of the old men asked.

"That's right," Grandpa answered. "His name is Ralph Boyd. He's a friend of Jess Wootley."

"I'd say they're two of a kind," said the old man. "Can't imagine Bill Lacy going off to California for the whole summer. And leaving Wootley in charge of his farm. Bet he didn't give him permission to let that Boyd fellow move in either. The two of them probably aren't doing any of the chores."

"Probably not," Grandpa said. "Neither one of them is worth much. But you know how soft Bill Lacy is. Wootley probably gave him a big sob story. And Bill fell for it."

Grandpa pushed back his hat and wiped his forehead with his big handkerchief. "I don't care what happens to those two," he said. "But it's the boy I worry about. I can't help feeling sorry for him."

"Boy?" asked the old man. "What boy?"

"Boyd's nephew," Grandpa answered. "He must be around 11 or 12. The two men pulled an old trailer house in on Lacy's place about three weeks ago.

Parked it alongside Wootley's cabin. Seems like the boy kind of takes care of himself. Guess he doesn't have any other folks. Been living in foster homes until his uncle took him in."

"I think he'd be better off anywhere than with those two bums," the old man said.

On the ride home, Louie and I pelted Grandpa with questions.

"Is Wootley the fat man?" I asked.

"That's right," Grandpa said.

"Where's Lacy's place?" Louie asked.

"Just down the road from us," said Grandpa. "On the other side of the tree farm."

"Are they dangerous?" I asked. "What if they . . ."

"Now hold on, hold on," Grandpa ordered. "They're just a couple of good-for-nothings. They don't bother us. And we don't bother them."

"It might be better if we didn't say anything to your grandma." Grandpa pulled into the driveway. "It would just upset her."

"That's a good idea," agreed Louie. "She gets pretty loud when she's upset."

3

Johnny Boyd

Louie and I had fun on Grandma and Grandpa's farm. I learned to churn butter, make strawberry shortcake, feed the chickens, clean the chicken coop, and gather the eggs. And Grandma had promised to teach me to make jelly and jam during the summer.

Louie was turning into a real little farmer. He finally got the hang of milking a cow. Still, he was pretty slow compared to Grandpa. It was hard to believe anyone's fingers could move as fast as Grandpa's when he milked.

Louie said he'd be able to milk as fast as Grandpa before long. But Grandpa said that would probably take longer than one summer vacation.

"Maybe Mom will have a baby again next year," said Louie. "Shall we ask her?"

Grandpa didn't answer. He just cleared his throat and changed the subject.

Louie learned about feeding the pigs and cleaning the barn. He even helped Grandpa build a new fence around the horse's pasture.

There was so much to do! And time went by so fast! It was more than two weeks before I realized that not once had I been Melanie Renee. All that time, I'd been enjoying myself being plain old Alice Martha. It was amazing!

Then Grandma finished the long dress! But not before we had a good dose of more excitement.

First, Louie caught a cold. And Grandma made him stay in bed. There was a good reason for his cold. Louie had gotten in trouble for the first time since we'd arrived at the farm. I hadn't really been watching him because he'd been with Grandpa just about every minute.

But the day before, Grandpa had gone to an auction

with some other farmers. And Louie was left home.

"I'm sorry it has to be like this, Louie," Grandpa said. "But it's going to be an all-day affair. And I'll be riding along with someone else. If I were taking my own pickup—"

"That's all right, Grandpa," Louie had said as though he really meant it. "I'll find something to do."

And did he ever!

Maybe it happened because Louie was angry. Or maybe it happened because he was bored. I think it was because it was just time for something to happen.

"Alice," Louie had said. "Let's build a pirate ship and go sailing on the duck pond."

"That's a dumb idea," I answered. "We don't have anything to build one with. We don't know how to build one. And even if we did, Grandma probably wouldn't let us. And who wants to anyway?"

Louie begged some more. I tried to get him to help me in the flower garden Grandma had let me plant. But he stomped off calling me horrible names. I should have kept my eye on him after that. But I didn't.

Louie found out how much work it was to build a pirate ship. So he gave it up. Instead he pried the wooden gate off the chicken run fence. He used a sheet that was hanging on the clothesline for a sail. And he sailed off across the pond.

It's a good thing I heard him yelling. Louie can't swim. This was the summer he was supposed to have started swimming lessons. He should have started them when he was six, the same as I did. But that was the summer he broke his arm trying to ride his bike on a railroad track. And then, Mom went and got pregnant and messed up this summer.

Louie may not have been able to swim. But anybody who could yell as loud as he could would never drown. Everyone within ten miles could hear him.

Grandma must have heard him too. She almost ran over the top of me on the way to the pond. I dived into the pond and swam faster than I ever had in my life. But I was scared. I was sure we would both drown.

And Grandma was certainly no help. All she did was stand on the bank screaming. "Alice, don't you dare let him drown! Please don't let him drown! You hear me?"

I wanted to tell her that she shouldn't have gotten so carried away with her scissors. Otherwise, I could've pulled Louie out by the hair. But now, I couldn't find a thing to grab. He had stripped down to his shorts. And they were twisted down around his ankles. Some pirate!

I finally got Louie out of the water. By then, he was naked and spitting out water like a whale. Grandma grabbed us both in a bear hug that pushed out whatever air was left in us. She was laughing and crying at the same time. Then she gave Louie quite a lecture.

It was bad enough that Louie almost drowned. And that he ruined one of Grandma's good sheets. But worst of all, all the chickens got out and took off in every direction.

They were in the garden, under the front porch, out in the road, and in the barn. One silly, half-grown rooster flew up in the lilac bush, threw back its head, and tried to crow. But all that came out was a sharp squawk that startled it. It lost its balance and fell into a rain barrel.

It took me more than two hours to round up all the chickens.

The next day, I asked Grandma if I could bake Louie some brownies. I felt sorry for him lying in bed, sneezing and sniffling—even if I was mad at him.

I was cutting the brownies into squares when Grandma came into the kitchen. She was carrying the new dress. In my whole life, I'd never seen anything so beautiful! It was blue with flowers. And it had a velvet sash around the waist. It was so gorgeous! It was a Melanie Renee dress!

I threw my arms around Grandma—as far as I could reach—and kissed her.

Grandma gave me a couple of quick pecks on the forehead, then pried me loose. "You get one spot on it," she warned. "Just one spot . . ."

I finished cleaning up the kitchen. Then I read to Louie until he fell asleep. Actually, he was so sniffly he didn't last very long. I read just a few pages.

I was glad. I rushed to put on the dress. Then I

sneaked out the front door and went for a walk. Grandma was busy out back, hoeing in her garden.

I held the long skirt up so I wouldn't get the hem dirty. I had never felt so unlike Alice Martha Turner. My drab brown hair turned golden. I became very dainty. And my freckles disappeared.

The first thing I knew, I was at the tree farm. I climbed up on a fallen log and looked out over the rows of trees. Only it was not a fallen log. It was the stage at Carnegie Hall. And the thousands of trees were the people in the audience clapping for the famous singer—Melanie Renee.

I pretended to wait for the applause to die down. Then I began to sing "Ciribiribin." It was a song I'd never heard until Miss Mackey, the music teacher, played it for the class. Most of the kids hated it and said it was dumb. But not me. I loved it—especially all the high notes.

I followed my first number with "Climb Every Mountain," my all-time favorite. My fans were spellbound. I sang louder and louder, waving my arms dramatically. I'm not sure how I really sounded when I sang. I heard my voice only the way I wanted it to sound. Oh, I was fantastic!

I was starting the second verse when I suddenly got the strangest feeling. It was the kind of feeling you get when someone is staring at you. I turned my head slightly. On the ground, not 20 feet away, sat a skinny, shaggy-haired boy wearing faded bib overalls and a tattered old hat.

I fell off the stage!

That horrible boy rolled all over the ground laughing. I grabbed the nearest thing handy—a fist-sized rock—and threw it at him. And I called him every nasty name I could think of.

The boy ducked and laughed harder.

I struggled to my feet, brushing evergreen needles from my dress. I had the feeling I'd seen that boy before.

"What do you think you're doing?" I shouted. "Sneaking up on a person like that?"

"I thought I heard a coyote caught in a trap," the boy snickered. "I came to save it."

"Very funny!" I snapped. "Very, very funny!"

Where had I seen that boy before? When he stood up, I saw how really tall and skinny he was. He walked toward me, took off his hat, and bowed idiotically. "Please, miss," he said. "May I have your autograph?"

I slapped the dirty hat from his hand. "I hate you!" I screamed until my throat hurt. "I hate you! Hate you! Hate you!"

That horrible boy started laughing all over again. Then I recognized him! He looked like Huckleberry Finn!

Suddenly I felt very foolish. I was standing there in my beautiful long dress being plain old Alice Martha

Turner. I was too tall and awkward, with drab brown hair and freckles. I was going to cry, I just knew I was. I blinked as fast and hard as I could. But a couple of tears squeezed out and rolled down my cheeks.

"Aw, come on," the boy said. "You don't have to cry, do you?"

"I'm not crying," I blubbered.

The boy twisted his long legs around and around. "Well, I'm sorry I laughed at you." A grin started at the corners of his mouth, then stopped. "But you did look kind of . . . well, I'm sorry."

"It's bad manners to sneak up on people," I sniffled.

"I didn't sneak up on you," the boy protested. "I was sitting there long before you came. I come here every day to watch the birds and the small animals. I put food out for them. I live right over there. On the Lacy place."

"The Lacy place?" I exploded, bringing a puzzled look to his face.

Oh! The poor boy! I thought. That awful man we saw in town that day is his uncle. No wonder he's so skinny. They probably starve him—his uncle and that fat Jess Wootley. And those ragged clothes! Probably the only ones he owns. Oh, the poor boy!

"What's your name?" I asked in my friendliest voice.

"Johnny Boyd," he replied.

"Hi, Johnny. I'm Alice Turner," I said brightly.

"That's my grandparents' farm over there. My little brother and I are spending the summer with them."

Johnny just stood there with a puzzled look on his face.

"Hey," I said. "You want to come to the house with me? We can have some brownies. I baked them myself."

He backed away. "No, thanks," Johnny said. "I'm not hungry. Honest."

He was scared to death. He must have thought I was leading him into a trap. That I had a big brother or someone ready to pounce on him and beat him up.

A few minutes ago, that might have been a great idea. But now that I knew who he was, I could almost forgive his disgusting conduct.

I grabbed him by the shirt sleeve. "Oh, come on," I said. "I'm not mad anymore. Besides, I guess I did look pretty silly."

At that, Johnny smiled and relaxed a little. "I really am sorry," he said.

By the time Johnny and I got to the house, I had completely convinced him that it wasn't a trick. He knew that I really wanted to be friends.

Johnny started trembling when he got inside the house. But all the food spread out on the kitchen table seemed to help him overcome his fear.

It was lunchtime. Grandpa was washing up at the kitchen sink. He had bought some calves at the auction. And he'd spent all morning building a calf run behind the barn.

Louie wouldn't be much help for a while.

"I guess I should've taken him along to the auction," Grandpa had said at breakfast. "Then I wouldn't have to build that calf run all alone."

Grandma was just coming out of the bedroom that Louie and I shared. When she saw Johnny, she stopped dead in her tracks.

Johnny flushed. He did look rather strange. His pant legs were rolled up to keep from dragging. There was only one button on his shirt. The only thing that fit right was his hat. And it was practically all holes.

"This is my new friend, Grandma," I said cheerfully. "His name is Johnny. And he lives on the Lacy place. May he eat with us?"

"Lacy place, huh?" Grandpa said. "You must be Ralph Boyd's nephew."

"Do you know my uncle?" Johnny asked in a meek voice.

Grandpa cleared his throat. "Not exactly," he said. "I've just heard of him."

Grandma cleared her throat too. But she didn't say anything. I could tell that Grandpa had decided to tell Grandma what had happened in town after all.

Johnny stood there looking taller and skinnier than ever.

Finally Grandma said, "Well, Johnny, you going to

just stand there growing through the ceiling? Or are you going to eat?"

Johnny ate. He ate as if he hadn't eaten in a week. Every time his plate got close to empty, Grandma filled it again. Even when it looked like Johnny was having trouble holding any more food, she kept shoving more at him.

Grandma didn't know it then. But she'd just elected herself president of the Fatten-Up-Johnny Club. Johnny was a guest at our table for just about every meal from then on.

4

Indian Hill

A couple of days later, Grandma let Louie get out of bed. She had decided his runny nose wasn't going to turn into pneumonia.

"Now stay out of trouble," Grandma warned.

"Don't worry," Louie said. "I will."

Louie hadn't met Johnny. But I'd told my brother all about him.

Of course, I was careful to leave out the embarrassing part of Johnny's and my first meeting. If Louie ever found out about that, he'd never let me live it down. It was bad enough having Johnny know. He hadn't once mentioned it since it happened. I guess he'd been too busy enjoying Grandma's cooking. She stuffed him every chance she got.

After the scene at the tree farm, I had packed the long dress away. I had decided that it just wasn't for me. Not for plain old Alice Martha Turner.

The night before, Mom had called to see how everything was going. I got all choked up when I heard her voice. I missed her more than I'd realized.

"Hi, honey," Mom began. "How are you?"

"Fine," I answered, swallowing hard. I told her how much fun Louie and I were having. And I said not to worry about us. I didn't tell her about the long dress or about Louie's almost drowning. I did tell her about Johnny. But I didn't tell her exactly how I had met him.

Mom giggled and said something silly about not losing my head.

"I really miss you two," said Mom. "I really do." She seemed pleased that we were having such a good time.

"I know I've been impossible, Alice," Mom said. "But after the baby comes, I'll make it up to you. You'll see."

I certainly hoped so. She had been great before she got pregnant. But that seemed so long ago.

Mom said she would call as soon as the baby was born. And she told me and Louie to be good, have fun, and help Grandma and Grandpa.

When Louie finally got to meet Johnny, he liked him. Johnny offered to take Louie and me fishing the first chance we had. Neither of us had ever been fishing before.

Grandpa had a couple of old poles in the attic. And he fixed them up for us.

"I haven't used these for so long," Grandpa said, "I'm not sure what shape they're in." He handed one to me and one to Louie. "But I guess they'll still work."

Grandpa offered to lend Johnny his good pole. But Johnny had his own. It looked as old and battered as everything else he owned. But Johnny said it was just fine. "It's not worn out," he explained. "It's just broken in."

I was afraid Grandma wouldn't let us go fishing with Johnny. But she was all for it. She packed us a great lunch.

"Now be careful," Grandma said. "And don't you dare come back empty-handed. My mouth is just watering for a mess of trout."

Louie sighed when we were out of sight of the house. "What if we don't catch anything?" he wondered aloud. "What will Grandma do?"

"Probably fry you," laughed Johnny. He slapped my brother on the back. "Don't worry about coming back empty-handed. I personally guarantee that we'll catch a mess of trout."

Louie breathed a sigh of relief and grinned up at our new friend.

Johnny was fun. I was glad I'd met him. I just wished it could have been under less embarrassing circumstances. And I wished it weren't just for the summer. Other boys, even Jeffrey Ober, would be pretty dull after Johnny.

"Where are we going fishing?" asked Louie as we trudged along through the pasture.

"Silver Creek," Johnny replied.

"Where's that?" I asked.

"Up on the game refuge," Johnny said.

Louie stopped dead still. His eyes looked like two big blue marbles ready to fall to the ground. "Game refuge!" he finally blurted out. "You mean the game refuge on Indian Hill?"

Johnny nodded and kept walking.

I couldn't help slowing down a little. But I didn't want Johnny to think I was scared.

"What about the ghost?" Louie cried from behind. "Aren't you afraid of it?"

"Ghost? What are you talking about?" Johnny asked.

"Don't you know about the Indian who's buried up there?" asked Louie. "It happened a long time ago. About a hundred years."

Johnny laughed. "Oh, that," he said. "Jess Wootley told me how the place got its name. But that doesn't mean there's a ghost running around up there. That's only a superstition. There's no such thing as ghosts."

Louie looked at me. If it was courage he was looking for, I couldn't help him any. But if Johnny wasn't scared, I'd try not to be either.

Johnny knew a lot about the country and the woods and animals. He liked animals so much, he was even hoping to be a vet someday. I thought that was an excellent idea. He'd be a good vet.

Johnny had told us that most of the places he had stayed since his parents died had been farms. He didn't call them foster homes. He said they were places where he'd worked.

One place had been a dairy. And Johnny had helped milk 20 cows, clean barns, and deliver calves. Johnny told about being knocked down and trampled by a cow. He'd been trying to get it in a pen because it was due to have a calf at any time.

"I've known pregnant women that mean," Louie said.

We followed Johnny to the edge of the pasture. And then we walked along a trail that climbed almost straight up.

Johnny explained that it was an animal trail. "Mostly deer," he said. "This trail heads straight to the pasture. The deer probably graze there every night."

"But how do they get over the fence?" asked Louie.

"Fences don't mean a thing to deer," Johnny said. "They sail right over the top of them. A fence would have to be more than ten feet high to keep a deer out."

It was beautiful up on Indian Hill. So beautiful that I could almost forget about the story Grandpa had told.

Louie didn't seem to be thinking about the ghost either. It was too beautiful to think about anything so horrible.

The houses and barns on the farms down in the valley looked like toy buildings. Even Grandma and Grandpa's place looked very small, though it wasn't that far away. I could see Grandma out in the yard watering the garden. I waved, but she didn't see me.

When we finally got to Silver Creek, Johnny showed Louie and me how to bait our hooks. I dreaded knowing that I'd have to do it by myself next time. I didn't mind handling the worms. It was watching them squirm on the hook that bothered me.

It was nice sitting on the bank under the trees. A cool breeze was blowing across the water. And it felt good.

There must have been a hundred birds in the trees. And Johnny knew the names of every one. He could make the sounds most of them made too. He even taught Louie and me a few.

"Hey, that's good!" Johnny exclaimed at my oriole call.

Louie's birdcall sounded more like a chicken with a cold. But Johnny didn't laugh.

A pair of squirrels played tag on a limb overhead. And later we saw a little brown rabbit hop out of the bushes and nibble some clover. Johnny said it was a cottontail. It didn't seem to mind our sitting there at all.

"It's like a zoo," Louie said. "The animals aren't even afraid."

"That's because they're protected here," explained Johnny. "They have never been hunted. So they have no fear of people. Only the caution that their natural instincts give them."

"You mean I could pick that rabbit up and take it home?" Louie asked.

"Probably not just like that," said Johnny. "And even if you could, it wouldn't be right. Wild animals should be left free."

I agreed with Johnny. I always felt sorry for the caged animals when Dad took Louie and me to the zoo. I thought how nice it would be to turn them all loose and let them go back where they belonged.

But Dad said the animals wouldn't know how to take care of themselves in the wild. They'd starve or be killed by other animals. But it was a lot nicer seeing the animals running free than seeing them in a zoo.

Johnny caught a fish right away. But Louie and I weren't having much luck. Actually, I was trying hard to make my worm last all day. I couldn't stand the thought of baiting my own hook.

"Be patient," Johnny told us when we began to complain. "It takes time and practice."

At noon, we stopped and ate the lunch Grandma had packed. We had ham sandwiches, hard-boiled eggs, cheese and crackers, and lemon cupcakes.

"Your grandmother has to be the world's best cook." Johnny crammed half of a sandwich into his mouth. I had never seen anyone with an appetite like Johnny's.

After lunch, we tossed some scraps of food a few feet away. In no time, the chipmunks and some scolding blue jays were having a feast.

We propped our poles on some forked sticks that Johnny had pushed into the ground. Then we leaned back against a log to enjoy the scenery. After a while, a pretty little doe stepped out into the clearing on the opposite bank. It stood very still and watched us.

"Don't move," Johnny whispered.

We watched. The doe's eyes kept getting bigger and bigger. And every so often, its nose twitched. For a long time, it stood perfectly still. Then suddenly it jerked and bounced off through the brush.

"Why'd it run off like that?" Louie asked.

"I don't know," Johnny answered. He looked around, puzzled. "Something must have spooked her."

"I didn't hear anything," I said. "Or see anything."

"Me neither," said Johnny. "But something scared

her. The way she took off, you'd think she'd seen a ghost."

"A ghost!" Louie gasped, flying to his feet. "Let's get out of here!"

Louie was all set to take off when Johnny grabbed his arm. "I didn't mean there's a ghost running around in the woods," he said. "That's only an expression."

But I was thinking the same thing Louie was. If it was a ghost, maybe we wouldn't have seen or heard it. But what about a deer? What about any animal? Weren't animals supposed to have a sixth sense or some such thing?

My friend Michelle had a dog that met her father's bus every day. How did he know what time the bus got there? And what about lost animals that have found their way back home? Some travel hundreds of miles. How could we know what the doe had seen or heard— or sensed?

"Listen," Johnny said. "If there really is a ghost around here, the animals wouldn't stay around. Right?"

Louie poked a million holes in that theory. "Maybe the ghost only shows up when people are around," he said. "It was people the Indian was mad at. Not animals."

Johnny didn't argue any more. I guess he figured it was useless. Louie was pretty stubborn.

It wasn't as much fun the rest of the day. Even though we saw a mother skunk and her babies. And

Louie and I each caught a fish. Mine was just barely big enough to keep. But it was a fish—and my first one. Johnny caught seven more.

Louie and I didn't talk much on the way back home.

Grandma was so excited over the fish. She gave Louie and me one of her bear hugs.

"Hug Johnny too, Grandma," said Louie. "He caught the most fish."

And so Grandma did—much to the embarrassment of Johnny. It surprised us all. Grandma was usually pretty stingy with her hugs. She saved them for special people and special occasions.

Grandma fried the fish for dinner. We also had lima beans with ham, salad, baked yams, hot rolls, and apple pie. Grandma insisted that Johnny eat the two biggest fish and the last piece of pie. He didn't argue.

It was a delicious meal. And the fresh air and long walk had made me extra hungry. But even so, I had a hard time keeping my mind on eating. I was wondering what had frightened the deer. I almost wished Grandpa had never told me the story about the Indian.

After dinner, Johnny and Louie helped Grandpa do the chores. And I helped Grandma in the kitchen.

I was getting so I could talk to Grandma a little better now. I'd discovered her bark was worse than her bite, as Dad had said.

I didn't want to come right out and ask Grandma about the Indian ghost story. I thought she'd scold me for being foolish. Or she might be mad at Grandpa for telling us. So I told her about the deer.

"None of us could figure out what made it act so strange," I said.

"Deer are nervous animals," Grandma said.

"But she wasn't scared of us," I argued.

"No need to be. She knew you wouldn't hurt her. Something else upset her, that's all."

I decided either Grandma didn't believe in ghosts. Or she didn't want to upset me. So I changed the subject.

"Grandma, do you think you could hem my long dress?" I asked. "You know, make it short?"

She gave me a quick, puzzled look.

"It would still be nice short," I added hurriedly.

"I thought you wanted a long dress," Grandma said in a sharp voice. "Now you don't like it?"

"Oh, I love it!" I exclaimed. "It's the most beautiful dress I've ever owned. But—well, that kind of dress is for someone more . . . more dainty. I'm not exactly dainty."

"And be thankful you're not!" Grandma snapped. "There's nothing more useless than a fluff of a girl who's good for nothing more than her looks!"

"But, Grandma," I whined. "I'm not pretty. And that long dress is for someone who is."

That was the wrong thing to say. Grandma hit the ceiling! She grabbed me by the shoulders.

And she shook me so hard I thought my teeth would fall out.

"There's no such thing as a little girl who isn't pretty!" she announced. "Some may be prettier than others. But you can hold your own with the best of them. And don't you ever forget it!"

Then Grandma gave me one last shake. "Now go wash up. When the boys get back from the barn, we'll talk your grandfather into taking us to a movie. It's time we did something different for a change."

"Johnny too?" I asked hopefully.

"Johnny too," said Grandma.

I looked at myself in the bathroom mirror. My freckles didn't look as dark as usual. My mouth didn't look as big. My hair didn't look as dull. I smiled at myself.

"I'm not pretty, Grandma," I whispered. "But I love you for saying so."

5

A Fox in a Box

The five of us got home from the movie a little after midnight. Grandpa drove into the Lacy driveway to drop off Johnny.

There were no lights on in the trailer house. Jess Wootley's cabin was dark too. There was an old car in the driveway. I figured it must belong to Johnny's uncle. But Jess Wootley's battered green pickup was nowhere around.

I felt sorry that Johnny had to be there all alone. But he didn't seem to mind. I guess he was used to it.

Grandma and Grandpa didn't say a word about Johnny's situation. But while I was in the bathroom getting ready for bed, I heard them talking in the kitchen.

Grandma had plenty to say about Ralph Boyd and Jess Wootley. They were good-for-nothings. And they had no business keeping Johnny.

Grandpa agreed, but in a quieter voice. "There ought to be a law against raising a boy that way," he said.

I agreed. I thought about my own family. Look how well our parents cared for Louie and me. They would never dream of leaving us all alone at night.

It was late when Louie and I finally went to bed. But we talked for a while before we went to sleep.

We talked about Johnny—about how much we liked him.

"How awful it must be for him not to have any family," I said. "Except for that crummy uncle who couldn't care less about him."

We talked about the new baby that was coming. Louie wanted it to be a boy.

"I could teach him how to play baseball and football!" Louie said. "I could teach him how to fish and hike and swim!"

"Swim!" I exclaimed. "You're going to teach him how to swim?"

"Well," Louie mumbled. "As soon as I get a little better, I can teach him." He sighed. "I can teach him lots of other things too."

I didn't care much. I just wanted the baby to hurry up and get here so Mom would feel better.

Louie and I talked about all the fun we were having on the farm. We talked about everything—except the frightened deer on Indian Hill and Grandpa's story.

I guess Louie and I were both thinking the same thing. Lying all alone in a dark room in the middle of the night was no time to be talking about ghosts. It was no time to be even thinking about ghosts.

As the days went by, I decided that I didn't want to go back to Indian Hill again. It wasn't just the deer's strange behavior that made me feel that way. It was also the story Grandpa had told us about the Indian.

I couldn't get that story out of my mind. I knew Grandpa didn't believe in ghosts. But I was pretty sure that I did. And I wasn't looking forward to running smack into one—especially one that had been angry for more than a hundred years.

Johnny didn't come over for several days. And we all started wondering what had happened to him. I knew Johnny liked all of us. And it wasn't like him to miss out on Grandma's cooking.

I wanted to go over and see what was wrong. But Grandma wouldn't let me.

"I don't want you anywhere near that place as long as the Lacys are gone," Grandma said. "I wouldn't be surprised if Johnny's worthless uncle has pulled out. Those kind of people never stay in one place very long. We very well may have seen the last of that poor boy."

I hoped not. I'd really gotten to like Johnny a lot. And I knew that Grandma was worried about him too.

"I was just starting to put a little meat on his bones," Grandma complained. "Over at his place, he'll be lucky if he gets a decent meal once a week."

I was bored without Johnny around. I started spending more time in my bedroom reading and listening to the radio. The rest of the summer wouldn't be much fun without Johnny. I even tried being Melanie Renee. But it had been so long that I was out of practice. And my heart just wasn't in it.

It wasn't so bad for Louie. He missed Johnny too. But he kept busy, and that helped. He spent most of his time with Grandpa doing things around the farm. When he wasn't helping Grandpa, he was under the house with Grandma's cat and her new kittens.

"I just don't understand it," Louie said. "Mom's cranky when she's expecting. And that dumb cat's cranky when she's not expecting."

"What kind of talk is that?" Grandma said, bandaging his scratched hand for the fifth time.

It was early one morning when Johnny finally showed up at the back door. He was carrying a cardboard box with holes cut in the sides. Grandma let him in. Then everybody started chattering all at once.

"Johnny!" my brother squealed. "Where have you been? We missed you. What's in the box?"

"It's about time you showed up," said Grandma. "We were so worried about—"

"What's in the box?" interrupted Louie.

"We thought you had moved away, Johnny," I said. "I wondered why you didn't tell us good-bye."

"What's in the box?" Louie persisted.

"Glad to see you're okay," Grandpa said. "We certainly did miss you. You've just about become one of the family."

"What's in the box?" Louie asked again.

Johnny grinned. "I didn't know I was so popular."

"For Pete's sake!" yelled Louie. "What's in the box?"

"Calm down and I'll show you," Johnny replied. He set the box on the floor. "This is why I haven't been around for a while. I've been busy playing doctor." He raised the lid halfway.

"Well, I'll be!" Grandpa exclaimed, kneeling down by the box. "A young fox. How did you ever manage to catch him?"

"He was hurt," Johnny said. "Hurt bad. Looked as though he had gotten into someone's chicken house and torn himself up." Johnny closed the lid on the box and glanced at Louie and me. "I'm going to let him go on Indian Hill. And I thought you two might want to come along."

I was so happy about seeing Johnny again. And for the moment, I forgot about being afraid of Indian Hill. So did Louie.

As Johnny, Louie, and I hiked up the hill, Louie chattered a mile a minute.

"The cat had kittens," Louie said. "Two girls and two boys. Grandpa and I built a toolbox for the tractor. And I painted it all by myself. I picked some berries. And Grandma made a cobbler. You didn't come, so Grandpa and I ate your share."

Johnny admitted that he hadn't had a good meal since he'd last been to our house. "Jess and Uncle Ralph aren't much for cooking," he said. "Besides, they're not home much. They spend most of their time in town. That's what kept me so busy. Taking care of the fox and doing all of the chores." He sighed and shifted the box in his arms. "Sure will be glad when the Lacys get back."

I was sorry that Johnny got stuck with most of the chores. But I secretly wished that the Lacys would never come back. Then maybe Johnny and his uncle would stay for good. If they did, I'd beg to come to Grandma and Grandpa's every summer.

Johnny turned the fox loose close to the spot where we'd gone fishing. "I've seen some foxes in this area a couple of times," said Johnny. "Maybe he'll run across his family."

"What if he doesn't?" I asked.

"He's old enough to take care of himself," Johnny answered. "Not much of anything will bother a fox, anyway."

We sat on a log and watched the fox for a long time. He was glad to be free. But he kept looking back at Johnny.

"Go do your own hunting," laughed Johnny. "I'm not your mother anymore."

The fox was limping a little. But Johnny said he thought he would be all right. "If he's penned up too long, he will forget how to take care of himself."

"I wish I could have him for a pet," I said.

"It's not good to make pets out of wild animals," said Johnny. "They need to be free. That's the way nature meant for it to be."

I knew Johnny was right. But the little fox was so cute. And he looked so cuddly.

When the fox started off, we followed to see which way he would go. He padded along the creek bank, stopping once to drink. We laughed at the way his little pink tongue slapped at the water.

After a while, the fox changed direction. He crossed a clearing and headed for a grove of young oak trees.

Again, the fox looked back over his shoulder at Johnny. He seemed to be trying to decide between his freedom and the one who had cared for him. He raised his head slightly and shook himself. Then once more, he headed toward the oak grove. He had made up his mind.

"Maybe he knows this area," Johnny said. "Let's follow him for a while and see where he goes."

Johnny led the way. Louie and I walked a short distance behind. Suddenly Johnny drew in his breath and raised a hand, motioning for us to stop.

"What's the matter?" Louie asked in a loud whisper.

Johnny put his finger to his lips.

"Quiet," he ordered. "I heard something."

We stood like statues and listened. All I could hear was a little breeze blowing and a bird singing. Then— just the breeze. The bird had stopped singing.

Then we heard dry leaves rustling. Someone or something was walking through the oak grove! The fox whirled around as a limb snapped loudly. And with one quick leap, he was out of sight.

The footsteps continued. The hairs on my arms stood up. I couldn't see Johnny's face because his back was to me. But if Louie's face had been any whiter, it would have been invisible. My heart was thunk-thunking in my chest. The footsteps were coming closer, right toward us.

Oh, how I hoped I wouldn't throw up! I had done

that once in the spook house at Jantzen Beach Park from getting so scared.

I tried to swallow. But the sides of my throat stuck together.

Then, of all things, Johnny called out, "Hello! Who's there?"

Had he gone stark, raving mad?

The footsteps stopped. There was dead silence. Louie edged closer to me. He was staring wide-eyed and trembling.

"Who's there?" Johnny called again.

Oh, why didn't he keep quiet? What was wrong with him, anyway?

The sound of the footsteps started once more—louder, then hard and fast. Someone was running, breaking limbs and crashing through brush.

I grabbed my brother and he grabbed me. Then we ran. I didn't know my legs could move so fast. It was like flying without leaving the ground.

When we finally came to a stop, I sprawled on the ground, panting. Finally, I caught my breath. "What do you think it was, Johnny?" I asked.

Johnny didn't answer. I looked up. He was nowhere around. There was only Louie, lying face down in the grass. If I hadn't been so frightened, I would have burst out laughing. He looked so ridiculous.

"Where's Johnny?" I asked.

Louie looked up from the grass. "I don't know," he

puffed. "I thought he was right behind us. You think we—we'd better go—look for him?"

"No way!" I exclaimed. "I'm not going back there!"

"But we can't leave him back there alone," Louie said. "We have to help him. Don't we?"

"What could we do anyway?" I asked. "We'll wait here. If he doesn't come in a few minutes, we'll go get Grandpa."

We waited for what seemed like hours. But it was really just a few minutes. Louie and I decided it was time to go for help. But just then, Johnny showed up.

"What the heck is wrong with you two?" Johnny asked. "You took off like a pair of scared rabbits."

Louie hung his head and looked a little ashamed. Personally, I couldn't see anything to be ashamed of. Only a dope wouldn't have taken off. There was no telling what was tramping around up there. And I told Johnny so.

"Someone was just walking in the woods," Johnny said. "The same as we were."

"How do you know it was a person?" I asked.

"Come on," Johnny said. "Don't start that ghost thing again."

"But it could have been a ghost," Louie insisted. He paused a moment as if he were thinking something over. "Or something else just as bad. Like a bear. Or a lion."

Johnny looked as though he were trying to keep a

straight face. "Sure, Louie," he said. "That's what it was. A lion. A big, mean lion. Running on its hind legs."

Louie didn't like being made fun of. "You think you know everything!" he howled. "You'd be sorry if it was a lion or a bear! Or if it was an Indian ghost!"

Louie was so angry he was ready to cry. I was afraid Johnny was going to start laughing. The way he did at me the first time we met. But he didn't.

"I'm sorry, Louie," Johnny stammered. "I shouldn't have teased you. It's just that I don't believe in ghosts. And even if there were a ghost running around here, what could it do?"

I didn't know. But I didn't want to hang around to find out. "Let's go," I suggested. "Grandma didn't expect us to stay this long. We'll really be in trouble."

"I want to go back and see if I can find the fox," said Johnny. "Just to make sure he's going to be all right."

"You're crazy if you think I'm going with you," I told him.

"Or me either," Louie said, getting to his feet.

"I'm going home," I said firmly. "Come on, Louie."

"Wait," Johnny said. He grabbed Louie's shoulder. "What are you so worked up about? All we know is that someone else was walking in the woods. What is there to be afraid of?"

"Plenty," said Louie. "If it was just someone walking in the woods, then how come he ran when you yelled?"

"Louie's right, you know," I added.

"I probably scared whoever it was when I hollered," Johnny answered.

"Yeah—well," stammered my brother. "That was still no reason for him to run."

"There was no reason for you to run either," Johnny said, a little smugly. "But you did. So what's the difference?"

For the life of me, I couldn't think of an answer.

Johnny patted Louie on the back. "Look, I've got a few chores to do back at my house," he said. "Then I'm coming back. Just long enough to see if the fox is okay. Why don't you run on home too. Then meet me back here in an hour."

There was no way I was going to go back in those woods. But then Johnny smiled at me.

"Okay, Alice?" Johnny said.

I didn't exactly melt or anything but . . .

"Well, okay," I said. "I guess. See you in an hour."

6

The Indian Ghost

An hour later, Louie and I met Johnny. I wore a new pink shirt and my best blue jeans. I'd brushed my hair until it shined. I thought I looked—well—pretty good. Grandma had even said so.

I didn't know what Johnny thought about how I looked. Or if he even noticed. The only thing he was concerned about was the fox.

Johnny was carrying a dead rat on a string. He'd caught it in the Lacys' barn.

"Yuck," I shuddered at the sight of it. "That's gross."

"To you maybe," said Johnny. "But not to the fox. Especially if he hasn't caught anything on his own yet."

Johnny had a pair of binoculars hanging around his neck. Louie begged to look through them.

"No way," said Johnny. "They belong to Jess Wootley. He doesn't even know I borrowed them. I have to make sure I get them back before he finds out they're gone."

I thought Johnny was crazy. But I didn't say anything. I sure wouldn't want to get Jess Wootley mad at me. I was scared to death of him and Johnny's uncle.

We hadn't walked very far before I noticed that something seemed strange. I couldn't quite put my finger on it. But I was wishing I were somewhere else instead of heading up to Indian Hill.

Indian Hill is a pretty name, I thought. I wondered about the Indian brave. He must have hated those white settlers a lot. And why not? He'd lost his whole family and many of his people because of the white settlers. He had every right to be angry. And in the stillness of the woods, I could almost feel his anger.

Suddenly, I realized what was so strange. The total stillness. Of all the times we had been in the woods, this was the first time it had been so still. Usually it was ringing with sounds. Today no birds were singing and no squirrels were scolding. The wind wasn't even rustling through the trees.

Oh, why had I agreed to come back? If I had it to do over again, Johnny could smile his fool head off. And it wouldn't change my mind.

And just what was wrong with Johnny anyway? It wasn't normal not to be scared of anything.

Johnny and Louie were walking a little ahead of me. I couldn't hear what they were talking about. But I could tell my brother wasn't as brave as he was pretending to be. He was walking as close to Johnny as he could without bumping into him.

I caught up with the two of them. Johnny stopped a couple of times. And he raised the binoculars to his eyes.

"I thought I might spot a Western tanager," Johnny said. "I saw one when I was here once before."

"What's a Western tan—tan—whatever?" my brother asked.

"A really pretty bird," said Johnny. "Something like an oriole." Then he stopped again and looked through the binoculars. "There's one now," he whispered.

Louie and I both looked up. I could barely make out a spot of yellow among the leaves.

Johnny lifted the strap over his head and handed the binoculars to Louie. "Now be careful," he whispered. "Hold on to—"

Johnny never got a chance to finish. At that moment, the most terrifying sound I'd ever heard in my life echoed through the woods. It sounded like someone or something in horrible pain.

I felt a lump the size of a golf ball pop up out of my chest and into my throat. It felt like I couldn't breathe. Goose bumps broke out all over my body.

Louie turned a funny kind of greenish-yellow color. I thought he was going to be sick all over the place.

"J-Johnny," I squeaked. "What—what was—"

But Johnny grabbed our hands. And we started running down the hill toward home. We didn't stop running until we reached the orchard. Then we fell on the ground. And all three of us lay there gasping for breath.

"I told you," Louie panted at last. "I told you. It was an Indian ghost."

"Indian ghost?" Johnny's voice was so low and deep I could hardly hear him. "What does an Indian ghost sound like?"

Louie let out a loud yell. "Just like that," he said. "Like what we heard."

"That's it!" I cried. "That's exactly what we heard." It was! I knew it was!

For the first time since I had known Johnny, he was speechless.

"Johnny?" I prodded.

"It could have been a . . ." Johnny stuttered, trying to think of something. "An owl. They sound kind of scary sometimes. An owl can really fool a person."

"If you thought it was an owl, how come you ran?" I asked.

"Because I knew you kids were scared!" Johnny snapped back. But then he sighed. "Okay, I admit it. I was scared too."

Johnny looked up toward the top of Indian Hill. He shook his head back and forth slowly. "I can't believe it," he said. "It can't be. I just can't believe it." He got up off the ground. "I have to go home." His face was as pale as Louie's. "I've got a lot of things to do."

For a long time, Louie and I sat there. We watched Johnny disappear from sight.

Finally, I stood up and brushed off my clothes. "Let's go, Louie," I said.

7

Bad Dreams

Dinner that night was quiet. Louie and I didn't have much of an appetite. And Grandma had fixed our favorite—spaghetti with meatballs. We were shoving the food around on our plates like it was brussels sprouts and liver.

Grandma stared at us. That didn't help matters any. I tried to swallow a meatball. But it would barely go past the golf ball that was still stuck in my throat.

"Is something wrong with the spaghetti?" Grandma asked. "Too salty? Too spicy? Not enough sauce?"

"It's really good, Grandma," said Louie. I nodded in agreement. "It's just that—"

"Apple pie for dessert, kids," Grandpa broke in. "With fresh whipped cream."

I wanted to throw up.

"That's it," Louie sort of groaned. "Apples. We ate about a hundred of them out in the orchard. Didn't we, Alice?"

Louie kicked me under the table. I backed him up in a hurry. "At least a hundred," I groaned. "Maybe two."

"Hmm," Grandma said. She stared at us for a few seconds. "You may be excused."

In our room that night, Louie and I made a promise. Under no circumstances would we tell Grandma and Grandpa about what had happened on Indian Hill.

That was my idea. Louie was all for dragging Grandpa right in on it. "Grandpa knows what to do about everything," he said.

But I convinced him not to tell.

In the middle of our discussion about the ghost, Louie fell asleep. He snorted a little in his sleep.

"Poor little kid," I whispered, pulling the covers over him.

I expected to lie awake half the night thinking of the ghost. But I didn't. I must have fallen asleep the minute my head hit the pillow.

But I dreamed. Did I ever dream! The most terrifying dream I'd ever had in my life.

I was on Indian Hill—all alone. I was at the Indian boy's grave. Then all of a sudden, the ground opened up. The Indian brave stood up and brushed away the dirt. He looked mad. And he started toward me.

But the worst thing was his body. It was covered with chicken pox. Giant chicken pox. I tried to run away. But he chased me. I ran faster. He ran faster. And as he ran, chunks of flesh fell from his body. Bigger and bigger chunks.

Finally, there was nothing left but a skeleton. The skeleton let out a bloodcurdling yell. I woke up screaming.

Louie groaned but didn't wake up. Luckily, neither did Grandma or Grandpa. It was a long time before I could get back to sleep. That was the most frightening nightmare I'd ever had.

The next morning, Grandma said I looked peaked. I didn't know what peaked meant. But I thought it must mean gross. That's because when I looked in the mirror, gross was what I saw. I looked just like Mom did when she had morning sickness.

I did manage to get some breakfast down. That made me feel better—a little.

Louie didn't look a whole lot better. But he was lucky. He had Grandpa to help take his mind off things. Louie had been helping around the farm so much he was actually developing muscles. At home, it was all Mom could do to get him to clean his room.

I hung around the house after Grandpa and Louie left for the barn. But that was a mistake. I got stuck helping Grandma with her canning.

I had helped Grandma can before—berries and fruit. That had been okay. Even fun. I could sneak a taste every time Grandma turned her back for a minute.

But now Grandma was canning green beans. I totally hated green beans. Having to help pick them was bad enough. But breaking them into pieces and dropping them into jars and just smelling them was the pits.

Grandma had the radio on. She was listening to some farm news and a cooking program. We didn't talk, so all I could do was think. And the one thing I did not want to think about was Indian Hill.

I tried playing Melanie Renee. But how do you pretend to be a beautiful movie star when you're elbow-deep in green beans?

I tried thinking about the new baby that was coming. Then I tried thinking about Grandma having a baby. I tried not to laugh out loud. As plump as Grandma was, it wasn't all that hard to picture. And, after all, she'd had three babies.

"Grandma," I said. "What's it like being pregnant?"

She jerked her head up at me. I thought she'd get whiplash. She stared a hole through me for a minute. Then she reached over and clicked off the radio.

"In what way do you mean, Alice?" she asked in a low voice.

She must have thought I was going to ask a lot of embarrassing questions. She kept taking deep breaths, preparing herself.

So I blurted out everything. About the weird junk Mom ate. About her temper tantrums. About the way she sat down and blubbered when I brought home the olives with no pits.

I couldn't believe it! My grandmother started laughing! She laughed so hard she had to sit down in a chair and hold her stomach.

"Oh, no!" Grandma said. "Mustard on pudding!" The tears streamed down her cheeks.

I had to laugh a little too—at Grandma.

But Grandma finally stopped laughing and motioned me to sit down. "Alice, let me tell you about when I was expecting your dad," she said. "I had only tasted chow mein once in my whole life. It had been when your grandpa and I were on our honeymoon.

"Well, in the middle of the night, I got the most awful craving for some chow mein," Grandma continued. "I just knew I'd go out of my mind if I didn't eat some.

"It was more than 15 miles to a town that had chow

mein," she said. "Clear over in Woodward. And it was pouring down rain. But your grandpa was so sweet about it. He got up and got dressed. And he said he'd be back in an hour."

Grandma chuckled and went on. "And he was. With a big carton of chow mein still nice and warm."

Then Grandma paused with a twinkle in her eye. I waited politely for her to continue.

"Well, Alice," Grandma said. "I took one look at that chow mein and got sick as a dog."

"Just like Mom!" I gasped.

"Oh, but that wasn't the half of it," Grandma continued. "Your grandfather was furious. He was soaked to the skin and tired. He reminded me that he'd driven 30 miles in the middle of the night in a rainstorm for the chow mein. And then he told me that I'd better eat it."

Grandma gave a big sigh. "Well, that did it. I picked up that carton of chow mein. And I threw it at him!"

"You didn't!" I howled.

"Yes, I did," said Grandma. "I can still see your grandpa. Bean sprouts in his hair. And chow mein juice running down his face."

I don't know when I'd laughed so hard. Grandma too.

After that, I felt a little closer to Grandma. It was nice.

Grandma and I started back on the green beans. Then we heard Johnny call through the back screen door.

"Hi," Johnny said. He looked about as bad as I did. He had dark circles under his eyes.

Grandma stopped the green bean canning. "I looked for you at breakfast," she said. "I had hot cinnamon rolls. I saved you some." She dragged Johnny to the table by his shirt sleeve. Then she pushed him into a chair. "You sit right down and I'll pour you some milk."

"I slept late," Johnny said. "I stayed up reading a book until midnight. Then I had a lot of chores to do this morning."

His excuse satisfied Grandma.

When Johnny finished eating, he and I headed outside. Grandma said she could finish the green beans.

"You've been a lot of help to me this morning," Grandma told me.

You've been a big help to me too, Grandma, I thought.

Out in the yard, Johnny stopped me. "We have to go back up Indian Hill," he said.

"Not on your life!" I shot back. "That was no owl. And you know it as well as I do!"

"I know that," Johnny said in a quiet voice. "But the binoculars. We left them up there. I have to get them before Jess sees that they're gone."

The binoculars! I had forgotten all about them. And it was Louie's fault they had been left behind. Johnny had just handed them to Louie when that terrifying scream filled the air. Louie must have dropped them.

There was no way out of it. We'd have to go back.

Johnny and I went to the barn to get Louie. We figured there was always safety in numbers. But Louie didn't want to go.

"I hate to think about what will happen when Jess finds out his binoculars are missing," Johnny said.

Louie gulped about five times. "Well, if I have to," he finally said.

I felt sorry for Louie. He didn't know who he was afraid of more—the ghost or Jess Wootley.

Johnny gave us a sort of pep talk before we took off. "Now here's what we have to do," he said. "We have to keep ourselves from thinking about—"

"We know," I said.

"Let's just concentrate on finding the binoculars," Johnny said. "And getting out of there as fast as we can."

"And never going back," Louie added.

Johnny nodded slowly. "Right. Never going back."

Johnny, Louie, and I didn't talk. We just marched up the hill. Johnny was in the lead. Louie was behind him. And I was last.

No matter how hard I tried, I couldn't keep from thinking about that noise and the ghost. I could feel little prickles on the back of my neck.

Then I remembered something terrible. We hadn't

told Grandma and Grandpa where we were going. What if we never came back?

Then a ridiculous thought crossed my mind. If anything happens to Louie and me, Mom will at least have the new baby. That made me feel sorry for myself.

I looked up. Louie and Johnny were far ahead of me now. They were almost out of sight.

"Hey, you guys!" I tried to yell in a whisper. "Wait for me!"

I started running to catch up. But I wasn't watching where I was going. I must have stepped into a hole or tripped over a branch. I was suddenly rolling head over heels. It seemed as though a million knives were jabbing into my ankle. It hurt so much.

After a few moments, I tried to stand up. But when my foot hit the ground, a million more knives stabbed me.

"Johnny! Louie!" I managed to call out.

They were completely out of sight. I was angry that they hadn't paid closer attention to me. But it was no use. They couldn't hear me, and I couldn't walk. I fell face down on the grass and cried. And on top of everything else, it started raining.

At first I thought I heard thunder. But it didn't sound quite right. I raised my head, blinked against the raindrops, and listened.

Was it a grouse? We'd heard a grouse one day. And

Grandpa said they made a rumbling noise by flapping their wings in the air really fast.

I listened some more. No, it wasn't a grouse. It was a different sound. And it was getting louder and faster.

Suddenly, I knew what it was. My heart nearly popped out between my ribs. It was a drum beating!

I worked myself into a sitting position. I was sitting on a lump. And something had gotten wrapped around my leg. It felt like a string.

I raised myself off the ground as far as I could. Then I pulled on the string with a jerk. A dead rat flew out from under me!

The violent shudder that went through my body smothered the scream in my throat.

8

Trapped Bobcat

When I woke up, I was in my bed. I could feel a bandage around my ankle. It was still throbbing. But it felt a lot better.

I saw my wet, muddy jeans and top draped over the back of a chair. Had Johnny and Louie dragged me all the way home? Later, I discovered bruises all over my body. And then I knew they had.

Grandma came in with soup, pudding, and a glass of milk on a tray. I gagged just looking at it.

"The boys told us how you sprained your ankle," Grandma said. "You must have passed out from the pain."

Louie and Johnny must not have told Grandma and Grandpa the rest of the story. And I guessed it was a good thing.

But maybe they should know, I thought. Especially since weird things were happening so close to their farm.

After a while, Grandma left. She took the tray with her. Then Louie came in. He said Johnny had gone home when he found out I was going to be all right. Louie still looked a little green. There were some scratches on his face.

"We fell down a hundred times trying to get you home," Louie said. "Boy, you weigh a ton!"

"Did you see anything?" I asked in a half-whisper.

"No," Louie answered. "But we sure heard it. Wasn't it freaky? That sound! Who else but that Indian ghost would have been beating that drum? It was probably buried in the grave with him."

Louie stopped, wild-eyed. He was scaring himself all over again.

"Well, anyway," Louie said. "I'm not going anywhere near that place again."

"Neither am I," I said firmly.

Grandma just about froze my foot off the rest of the day. She kept putting ice on it. But the swelling was going down.

I dozed off several times during the day. But every time I did, I had a nightmare. I really kept poor Grandma running.

Once, Grandma sat on the edge of my bed. She held my hand so I could sleep for a while without waking up screaming.

"I can't understand why you keep having bad dreams," Grandma said. "I guess it must be the pain."

"I guess so," I said. I felt so ashamed keeping things from her and Grandpa. But if we told them, they'd think we imagined the whole thing. After all, what proof did we have? None. Absolutely none.

I ate a pretty good dinner that night. Later on, I lay in my room with the door shut, just resting.

Louie was in the living room watching TV with Grandpa. I could hear Grandma in the kitchen. She was still canning. Poor Grandma. I had really fouled up her day.

It was just starting to get dark outside, though it wasn't all that late. My eyes were closed. A sound at the bedroom window made me sit straight up. It was a rustling sound. It sounded like something moving in the lilac bush.

With my eyes wide open, I peered toward the window. In the growing darkness, I could see the outline of someone standing there. I breathed in, trying to gasp enough air for a scream. But the gasp of air just jammed in my throat.

Then, over the pounding in my lungs, I heard a voice. It was a deep, echoing voice. "Aaaalice! Aaaalice!"

Oh, no! I thought in total hysteria. He—he knows my name! He's coming after me. Just like in the dream. I couldn't move. I couldn't even swallow.

The voice came again, a little louder. "Alice! Hey, it's me. Johnny."

I breathed out so hard it hurt. I lost every ounce of strength in my body and sunk back on the bed.

"Johnny!" I blurted. "You—you scared me half to death!"

"I'm sorry." Johnny opened the window far enough to stick in his head. "I had to let someone know. I'm going back to Indian Hill first thing in the morning. If I don't get back by 8:00—"

"Have you lost your marbles?" I interrupted. "You'd go back after what happened?"

"Not because I want to," Johnny groaned. "Jess discovered that his binoculars are gone. Right now he's accusing Uncle Ralph of stealing and selling them. But when he finds out . . ." He stopped with a shudder.

I gave a loud sigh. Oh, how I wished I didn't have to say what I knew I had to say. "Then—then I'm going with you," I said.

"You can't," Johnny said. "Not with your sprained ankle."

I knew I had a perfectly good excuse for not going. But I'd die if I let Johnny go alone and something happened to him.

"Wait to go until later in the day tomorrow," I said. "My ankle will probably be okay by then. It's a lot better already."

Johnny paused for a long time. "Well, I'll wait if I can keep Jess from killing Uncle Ralph. Or me." He grinned. "To tell the truth, I'd feel a lot better with someone along. I never thought I'd see the day when I'd be scared of a ghost."

"Now, about Louie," Johnny continued. "He may not want to go. But why don't we ask him anyway?"

So I talked to Louie later that evening. He did not want to go.

"I won't go!" Louie declared. "I won't go! I won't go! I won't! And you can't make me!"

I wanted him to go. I had become a great believer in the theory of safety in numbers. Even if one of those numbers was only a seven-year-old kid.

So I tried to shame Louie. I reminded him that he was the one who'd lost the binoculars. But that did no good.

"So?" Louie said. "I'll save my allowance and buy him another pair."

Louie didn't realize that it would take ten years to save that kind of money.

The next day, Grandma wanted to keep me in bed. But Grandpa told her that exercise might be good for my ankle.

Johnny came over in the morning and just hung around our place. Naturally, he ate lunch with us.

Then it was time to leave. Johnny and I didn't tell Grandma where we were going. We just took off. Louie followed us as far as the orchard, reminding us every step of the way how stupid we were.

"You wouldn't catch me going up there for a million dollars," Louie informed us as he turned to go back.

Johnny took a few steps, then stopped. "Maybe Louie is right," he said with a big sigh. "It's not too smart going up there alone." He called Louie back. "Go tell your grandpa where we're going. And ask him if he thinks that maybe he should come with us. And tell him everything."

I felt a little funny about sending Louie back to the farm by himself. Maybe we all should go and make one big confession. But then we decided that if we did, Grandpa would probably talk us out of going back to Indian Hill. Or he would simply forbid us to go at all. If we sent Louie by himself to tell our story, the chances were better that Grandpa would come to help us.

After Louie left, Johnny and I started walking slowly. We looked back every few minutes.

"Oh, why doesn't Grandpa hurry?" I said.

"He'll be along," said Johnny. "He was probably in the middle of something. But he'll be along."

If he even believes that Louie is telling the truth, I thought.

Johnny and I walked all the way to the place where we had gone fishing. And still no Grandpa.

"He'll be along," Johnny insisted.

I was beginning to get nervous. And I kept thinking about the other times we'd been on Indian Hill.

"Let's just sit here and wait," Johnny said as he sat down.

I sat next to him—closer than I meant to. But I wasn't about to move. We were on the opposite bank from where we had seen the deer. It was where Johnny had turned the fox loose.

"Be really quiet for a while," Johnny said almost in my ear. "And we might see the fox. If he's still around."

"I hope he's getting along all right," I said.

"He probably is," Johnny said. "By now he may not even remember me."

But Johnny was wrong. We'd only been there about two minutes when we saw the fox. He poked his head out from behind a rock.

"Hey, fella," Johnny called. "How are you doing?"

At the sound of Johnny's voice, the fox came out into the open. Johnny reached into his pocket. He pulled out a piece of bacon he'd wrapped in his handkerchief. And he tossed it onto the ground.

The fox slowly walked toward the bacon. He sniffed at it for a minute. Then he looked at Johnny. I had to giggle at the curious look on his face.

"Okay," Johnny laughed. "So it isn't steak. But it's better than nothing."

The bacon must have been all right. The fox picked it up in his teeth and disappeared behind the rock pile.

I was just getting ready to say, "Oh, what's keeping Grandpa?" when we heard another sound. It was coming from a thicket of brush a short distance down the creek bank. I leaned closer to Johnny. He didn't even notice.

"Let's check it out," said Johnny.

I held on to Johnny's arm. "Don't be crazy," I answered.

Johnny jerked loose. "Come on," he said. "It's only an animal digging. I can tell by the sound. Probably digging for grubs in a log. Maybe we can watch it."

I followed against my will. "What if it's a bear?" I asked in a very low voice. "I'm not sure I want to watch."

"It sounds like something smaller," said Johnny. "Like a raccoon. There are lots of raccoons along the creek bank. Or maybe a porcupine. Or a . . ."

Then the sound got really loud. But when we got closer, it stopped completely. Johnny motioned for me to freeze.

After a while, the noise started again. Only this

time, there was another noise too. It sounded like Grandma's old cat when she hissed at Louie for trying to pick up her kittens. Maybe that was it. Maybe she had packed her kittens off and hidden them to get away from Louie.

Johnny picked up a long stick and moved slowly toward the thick brush. The noise stopped again. He pushed the stick into the bushes and raised the limbs.

"Holy cow!" Johnny shouted. "Look at this!"

I crept closer and peered into the brush. It was a cat all right. But it wasn't Grandma's cat. It was a bobcat. And it was in a box. The box was made of rough wooden boards on two sides and heavy wire on the other sides.

"What's he doing in there?" I wanted to know.

"It's a trap," said Johnny. "It went inside after the bait. Probably a chunk of meat. Then the door snapped shut and it couldn't get out."

The poor bobcat was terrified. It scrunched down in the corner, trembling and slobbering at the mouth. Johnny said it wasn't very old. Not much more than a kitten.

"Can't we turn it loose?" I asked.

"Not yet," said Johnny. "Let's look around."

Johnny found another trap not too far from the creek bank. This one was empty. And the spring door was propped up with a stick.

"Look," said Johnny, kneeling down close to the box. "See these?"

Several rusty old nails had been bent over inside the box. There were hair and something like reddish-brown paint on them.

"Blood," said Johnny. "That must be what happened to our fox. It got into the trap and tore himself up on the nails. And somehow, it managed to get out."

I pointed to a dirty-looking rag inside the box. It was near a piece of fresh meat. "What's that?" I wondered.

"I'd say it's fox scent," Johnny answered. "I've read about things like this. You soak a rag in a special liquid. And it makes the rag smell like a fox. Only an animal can smell it." He looked at me. "Remember the deer? How weird she acted? That must have been what spooked her. She got a whiff of it and thought a fox was near. There's probably cat scent in the other trap."

Johnny laughed out loud. "Indian ghost!" he chuckled. "Oh, brother!"

"Why would someone be catching animals in traps?" I asked.

"That's what we're going to find out," Johnny answered quickly.

"I think we'd better get out of here," I said. "Let's go find Grandpa."

But it was too late! Someone was coming! Johnny and I heard feet shuffling through the dry leaves on the ground.

"Get behind that log over there," Johnny ordered in a loud whisper.

I was already halfway there.

"Now keep still," Johnny cautioned. "Don't move. Don't even breathe."

As whoever it was got closer, Johnny and I could hear voices.

"You sure you got rid of those darned kids?" asked a man's voice.

"Absolutely!" laughed another man. "They're probably still running."

"You'd better be right," the first one said roughly. "They come snooping around here again, and they'll get something they're not looking for."

I shuddered and let out my breath. Johnny clapped his hand over my mouth. "Quiet!" he hissed.

"Well, looky here!" said one of the men. "We got ourselves a little cat."

"Let's take a peek," Johnny whispered. "But be careful. If they catch us . . ."

Johnny didn't need to finish. We raised our heads slowly.

Luckily, the two men were facing the other way. One man was short and fat. He was squatting by the trap. A tall, thin man looked over the first one's shoulder.

I heard Johnny draw in his breath. "I should have known," he muttered. "I should have known all along!

How could I be so dumb?"

It was Jess Wootley and Ralph Boyd! Johnny and I slumped back down behind the log.

"We'll take this one back to the shed and empty it," said Jess. "Then we'll come back and check the others."

Finally, the sound of their footsteps faded away.

"Let's get to your place fast," Johnny said. "And we'll call the sheriff before Jess and Ralph get back."

I hobbled along behind Johnny. When we were halfway down the hill, I lost my balance. I fell into a clump of bushes. But instead of hitting the ground, I landed on something else.

Johnny helped me up. Then I pulled whatever I'd landed on from the bushes.

"Well, I'll be!" Johnny gasped.

It was a drum! It was brown with brightly colored designs on it. Johnny turned it upside down. A sticker on the bottom said "Made in Korea."

9

Melanie Renee

Johnny and I met Louie and Grandpa in the orchard. They were on their way to help us. Grandpa was shuffling along behind Louie.

"I couldn't help it," Louie explained. "I couldn't find Grandpa. After lunch, he went to a neighbor's house. He needed to borrow some tools."

Johnny and I both told the story. Then we all hurried back to the house.

Grandpa called the sheriff. I told Grandma about all the happenings of the past few weeks. I thought she was going to have a heart attack.

Johnny, Louie, and I begged to go with Grandpa and the sheriff. They were going to sneak up to Indian Hill. Then they were going to wait for Jess Wootley and Johnny's uncle. But Grandma wouldn't hear of us kids going along.

"It's too dangerous and you know it," Grandma said.

"Will we get a reward, Grandma?" Louie asked.

"Of course you won't get a reward," Grandma scolded. "You don't need a reward for doing what's right."

"But we were brave, weren't we?" Louie asked. "Especially Johnny and Alice."

"Brave—or just plain reckless," Grandma answered. "I'm not sure which. If it hadn't been for Johnny watching out for you, no telling what would have happened."

There Grandma went again, favoring Johnny. You'd think he was her grandchild instead of Louie and me. But I didn't really mind. If Johnny ever needed a friend, it was now.

I wanted so badly to ask what would happen to Johnny now. But I was afraid of the answer.

Jess Wootley and Johnny's uncle got caught in the act. The sheriff and Grandpa were waiting for them. The sheriff handcuffed them and took them off to jail.

After Grandpa got back, there was plenty of exciting news to tell. And it took Grandma twice as long as usual to finish cooking dinner. Actually, I didn't think I'd be able to eat a bite. But once I started, I almost outdid Johnny.

"Grandpa, what's going to happen to Mr. Wootley and Mr. Boyd?" Louie asked with a mouthful of dumpling.

"There'll be a trial, of course," Grandpa answered. "Then I suppose they'll spend some time in jail."

"A good place for both of them," said Grandma. "Even if one of them is Johnny's uncle."

Grandpa reached out and squeezed Johnny's arm.

"It's all right," said Johnny. "Uncle Ralph is getting what he deserves. He's not really my uncle anyway."

Grandma, Grandpa, Louie, and I all stared at him.

"Uncle Ralph used to be married to my mother's sister," Johnny revealed. "But she died a long time ago. There was a little insurance money when my parents died. So Ralph took me in. And after the money was gone, he put me in a foster home."

Grandma reached across the table and squeezed his other arm.

"Then, a while back," Johnny continued, "Uncle Ralph came and got me again. I never knew why."

"I suppose Ralph thought he'd use you in one of his little schemes," Grandpa said. "From what the sheriff found out, he's been involved in several. He has quite a record."

"But, Johnny," I said. "You and your uncle have the same last name."

Johnny flushed a little. "I thought if I used his name, it would make me feel like I belonged to someone," he said.

I thought I was going to cry. Grandma got up to pour coffee. I heard her sniffling.

"What were Jess and Uncle Ralph doing with those animals?" Johnny asked at last.

"They had quite a little business going," said Grandpa. "Jess dreamed it up after Lacy took off and left him in charge of the farm. And Boyd went right along with it. They were selling the animals."

"They were?" exclaimed Louie. "But you can't sell wild animals. They belong to everyone."

"Yes," said Grandpa. "It usually is against the law to sell or own wild animals. But a lot of rich folks buy them for private zoos. And sometimes ranchers will buy fur-bearing animals."

"You mean they were killing some of the animals for their furs?" I cried. "That's what would have happened to our fox if it hadn't got away!"

"I hope they hang them!" shouted Louie angrily.

"Now, Louie," said Grandma. "That's no way to talk."

But I could tell she was every bit as angry as Louie.

After dinner, a woman named Ms. Firth from the Welfare Department came to the house. She said the sheriff had called and told her about the arrests.

"I was sent to pick up a boy named John Boyd," Ms. Firth said.

Grandma jumped in front of Johnny. "You're not taking this boy!" she said firmly. "He didn't do anything. And he's not responsible for his uncle's behavior."

Ms. Firth smiled. But she looked a little startled. I didn't blame her one bit. Grandma looked ferocious.

"You don't understand, Mrs. Turner," Ms. Firth said. "We have to find a place for Johnny to stay. The boy has no home."

"Johnny's going to live right here with us," Grandma said. She shot a glance at Grandpa. "Isn't that right?"

Grandpa sputtered a few times. "That's—that's right," he finally said.

"You mean you'd like to apply to be foster parents?" asked Ms. Firth.

"If that's what it takes," Grandpa said. "Let's get started on it right away."

"I think that's a very good idea," Ms. Firth

answered. She smiled at Grandma as she backed toward the door. "I don't think anyone could be more—uh—concerned about his welfare."

When the door closed, Louie and I cheered. Johnny just stood there grinning from ear to ear.

"And we'll be coming this year for Thanksgiving," I cried. "Won't that be great?"

It seemed that everything was happening at once. That evening, Mom called from the hospital. The baby had been born early that morning.

"It's a girl, Alice!" Mom said, laughing and crying all at once. "A beautiful little girl. Oh, I wish you could see her."

"That's great, Mom!" I gushed over the phone. "I miss you, Mom. I can hardly wait to see you and Dad and the baby."

Mom said that Dad would come for us Saturday. I felt glad and sad all at once. I was dying to see Mom and the baby. But I'd really miss Grandma and Grandpa—and Johnny.

Mom talked to Grandma and Louie. And then she asked to talk to me again.

"Alice," Mom said. "I have a big surprise for you. We named the baby Melanie Renee!"

I almost dropped the phone. The room began to spin.

Oh, Mom, I thought. How could you?

"Alice! Alice!" Mom's voice was echoing in my ear.

"That's—that's nice, Mom," I sighed. "That's—real nice."

"I knew you'd be happy, honey," Mom said. "I know how much you love that name."

My hand was shaking as I hung up the phone. I just hoped I'd love my baby sister.

The next day, Johnny, Louie, and I went on a picnic. Grandma made so much lunch we had to pack it in two baskets.

It was more beautiful than ever on Indian Hill. It was hard to believe that such terrible things had happened there.

We caught a glimpse of our fox. But he didn't come toward us this time. When Johnny called out to him, he ran away.

"He's remembered he's a wild animal," Johnny said. "That's the way it should be."

I shuddered to think how close he'd come to being a fur coat or a caged pet.

The three of us went all the way to the top of the hill. It was the first time for Louie and me. I felt as if we were on top of the world.

"I'll show you something," Johnny said. "If you promise not to be scared."

Louie and I promised.

We followed Johnny to a peaceful-looking spot in a green, grassy clearing. A lot of pretty wildflowers were growing there.

"There," Johnny said. "There's your Indian ghost."

It was the grave. There was a marker on it. But the words were too faded to read. I felt all shivery. But not because I was scared. I was sorry about what had happened to the Indian and his people. Even if it had been a long time ago.

We picked wildflowers and put them on the grave. I said a little secret prayer for the Indian brave. Then we walked back to our favorite place by the creek and ate lunch.

Saturday came before I realized it. It was good to see Dad. I waited for Louie to get through jumping all over him. Then I introduced Dad to Johnny.

"You've both grown a foot taller," Dad said to Louie.

Grandpa filled Dad in on all the details of our summer adventure. And Johnny carried our things out to the car.

I got all choked up when Grandma gave me a hug and kiss. I cried. So did Grandma—a little.

Louie scampered off to the car after Dad. But I hung back so I could say good-bye to Johnny alone. Finally, I turned to leave.

"Ali," Johnny said. "Would you do me a favor?"

I whirled around in surprise. "What did you call me?"

Johnny twisted around like a pretzel. The way he does when he's uncomfortable. "Uh—Ali," he repeated. "I think it's kind of cute. And it fits you."

"Really?" I practically screamed.

Johnny flushed and twisted some more. "Well—anyway, when you come at Thanksgiving, will you wear the dress?" he asked. "The one you were wearing that first day?"

I stared, open-mouthed. I didn't know what to say.

"You looked real nice in it," Johnny said.

Oh, how I wished I had the nerve! I'd throw my arms around Johnny's neck and give him a big, fat kiss. But I didn't. So I just nodded and ran to the car.

I was excited to get home and see my baby sister—Melanie Renee.